The Drifting Away

The Drifting
Away

Poems by Leon Stokesbury

THE UNIVERSITY OF ARKANSAS PRESS   Fayetteville   1986

Copyright © 1986 by Leon Stokesbury
All rights reserved
Manufactured in the United States of America
Designer: Patricia Douglas Crowder
Typeface: Linotron 202 Trump Mediaeval
Typesetter: G & S Typesetters, Inc.

Grateful acknowledgment is made to the following publications in which some of the poems in *The Drifting Away* originally appeared: *Barataria Review, Carolina Quarterly, Mill Mountain Review, Mississippi Review, New England Review and Breadloaf Quarterly, New Orleans Review, New Virginia Review, The New Yorker, The Pacific Review, Poetry Northwest, Prairie Schooner, Quarterly West, Quartet Magazine, Red Weather, Shenandoah, Southern Poetry Review, The Southern Review,* and *Swallow's Tale.*

The poems, "As Many Think," "Gifts," "Little Keats Soliloquy," "Often in Different Landscapes," "Summer in Fairbanks," "The Lamar Tech Football Team Has Won Its Game," "The Murder of Gonzago and His Friends," "The North Slope," "This Print of Dürer's," "To All Those Considering Coming to Fayetteville," "To His Book," "To Laura Phelan: 1880–1906," and "What It Feels Like to Live in This Country to Me," some in slightly different versions, are reprinted from *Often in Different Landscapes* (University of Texas Press, 1976).

LIBRARY OF CONGRESS CATALOGING-IN-PUBLICATION DATA
Stokesbury, Leon, 1945–
   The Drifting Away.
   I. Title.
ISBN 0-938626-51-5
ISBN 0-938626-52-3 (paper)

for Susan

Contents

The stars was shining, and the leaves rustled in the woods ever so mournful; and I heard an owl, away off, who-whooing about somebody that was dead, and a whippowill and a dog crying about somebody that was going to die, and the wind was trying to whisper something to me and I couldn't make out what it was . . .

—THE ADVENTURES OF HUCKLEBERRY FINN

A Funny Joke

A man fell out of grace.
It was my father.

On the north slope of Alaska,
on land belonging to

the Atlantic-Richfield Oil Corporation,
he fell.

He lay there six hours.
Then he was found.

Three hours later,
the Atlantic-Richfield Oil Corporation

flew him to Fairbanks
where doctors were.

They said he was ill.
They said the way

his face, arm, leg, in fact
his whole left side

was drawn up
in a hideous, contorted,

spasm of paralysis
meant he was in ill health.

My brother was there.
My brother said

this was what was in my father's eyes:
fear.

My brother said
his mouth was twisted

into a permanent ghastly grin.
It looked always as if

his was the only smile around,
as if someone had told

the funniest joke finally,
but only he had heard

and we were unaware,
there, that last day

my father was an employee
of the Atlantic-Richfield Oil Corporation.

As Many Think

Occasionally, I've thought it would be good
to fix the world. Just last week, I saw
a man with his brain splattered all over
the road. The brain is not gray, as many
think, but more a pinkish with streaks of white
and red. Or maybe that was just the mess;
who could tell? Anyway, in Oklahoma City
a man who built a one-mile-square housing
addition explained they were all alike, except
"the garage and bathrooms, which are switched around
so people won't think they're all the same." And
Alice, married to Tom, cried late one night
"I love him but I think he hates my guts!" At which
I got out of bed to take a leak. Christ. And I would try
to fix all this—set my sign in the stars, so to speak. If
only it weren't so long it's been this way.
So many centuries it keeps just hanging here,
a dark shirt in a black closet,
waiting forever for something to fill it up.

Adventures in Bronze

At the Waldron Court Apartments
a young mother takes her toddler
into the living room to play,
then returns to the kitchen
to iron, and listen
to *Stella Dallas* on the radio.

Now the little one pushes at the front screen door,
finds it open, so stumbles out into the sun
where seven slightly older kids
come along, allowing him
to follow them
down the walk, down the road
to the old abandoned junior high
and the enormous, sunken, concrete storm drain there—
concrete smooth and cool,
concrete in the shade,
dark concrete the color
of Robert Oppenheimer's eyes
at any given moment in 1945.

The children climb down, scream, run around,
and so, with help, does the toddler too.
But then the older kids
climb out and run away,
climb out and leave the toddler alone.

The tips of his fingers can almost touch
the dead yellow grass
at the ground level top of the drain.

Soon enough he sees
there is nothing to do
except sit down on concrete and cry.

Soon enough he feels
there is nothing on earth
for him but this gray
and that blue rectangular swatch of sky.

From far far down the black tube of time
a man studies this scene in bronze.

A bronzed toddler is crying,
then looks up, seeing
first the head, then shoulders,
then the bronzed pedalpushers
of a bronzed mother there.

The man does not remember
the arms reaching up, or the arms reaching down,
just the distant sensation—
mendicant,
supplicant—
that he is risen,
that he inherits the air.

Unsent Message to My Brother in His Pain

Please do not die now. Listen.
Yesterday, storm clouds rolled
out of the west like thick muscles.
Lightning bloomed. Such a sideshow
of colors. You should have seen it.
A woman watched with me, then we slept.
Then, when I woke first, I saw
in her face that rest is possible.
The sky, it suddenly seems
important to tell you, the sky
was pink as a shell. Listen
to me. People orbit the moon now.
They must look like flies around
Fatty Arbuckle's head, that new
and that strange. My fellow American,
I bought a French cookbook. In it
are hundreds and hundreds of recipes.
If you come to see me, I shit you not,
we will cook with wine. Listen
to me. Listen to me, my brother,
please don't go. Take a later flight,
a later train. Another look around.

Renoir

Under the red-and-white striped awning
extended over the restaurant porch,
the eyelids of these fourteen sundry revelers

seem to sag a bit, and that is because
by now they are all just a little drunk.
The party is as parties are. The people

are talking. Laughing. But in the upper
left-hand corner, a man wearing
a saffron straw hat, tilted jauntily down

over his brow, stands slightly apart
and silent against the thin balustrade.
This man stands with his back arched,

his chest out, and the large muscles
in his bare arms self-consciously flexed.
Certainly, he cannot be at ease, but then those

who desperately hope to be loved rarely are.
I say this because if one follows
the man's gaze across the top of the canvas,

across the party, to the upper right-hand corner,
one sees that he is, I believe, staring
at a young woman who has raised her hands

to adjust her hat or her hair, or to cover her ears
so as not to hear what the two men talking
to her are saying. The two men are smiling,

and one has taken the liberty of slipping
his arm round her waist. The young woman
is the only person in the boating party being

physically touched, and though she seems
oblivious to it, the man in the saffron hat
is not, and is not much amused by it either.

Then, as the eye roams over the rest
of the festive scene, the quiet joke of the artist
begins to emerge. For, although a half dozen

conversations continue on, half of these people
are not even seeing the person looking at them.
They are looking at somebody else. It is a sort

of visual quadrille, the theme of five hundred
French farces, except in this case the painter
must care very much for them all, for he has soothed

their wants and aches in a wash of softness.
I think he must have been a little drunk too.
But it is the eyes, these misty, wine-dark eyes

of the three women in the center of the painting,
that draw a viewer back again and again.
The women are looking at men. They are looking

that way women sometimes look
when they have had a little wine, and when
they are listening to someone in whose presence

they see no reason to be other than who they are,
someone to whom, as a matter of fact,
they wish to communicate how simple and gentle

life can sometimes be, how amniotic even,
as it seems to them now. It is not clear
if the men of the boating party perceive this,

or anything. To be honest, they seem selfish and vain.
But the artist sees it. And this is his gift,
this warm afternoon, his funny story to tell again

and again: a day of blue grapes and black wine, of tricks
of the eye, of the flow and lulls of time, and everything,
everything soaked in the light of sex and love and the sun.

To Laura Phelan: 1880–1906

for James Whitehead

Drunk I have been. And drunk I was that night
I lugged your stone across the other graves,
to set you up a hundred yards away.
Flowers I found, then. Drunk I have been.
And am, standing here with no moon to spill
on the letters of your name; my loud fingers
feeling them out. The stone is mossed over.
And why must I bring myself in the dark
to stand here among the sour grasses
that stain my white jeans? Drunk I have been.
See, the thick dew slides on the trees, wet weeds,
wetness smears the air; and a vague surf
of wildflowers pushes my feet, slipping
close to my legs. When the thought comes at last
that people fall apart, that the things we do
will not do. Ends. Then, we come to scenes
like this. This scene of you. You apart:
this is not you; and yet, this is where I stand
and close my eyes, and feel the ragged wind
blow red and maul my hair. In the night somewhere,
dandelions foam. This is not you. Drunk
I have been. Across this graveyard, that
is where you are. Yet I stand here. Would ask
things of your name. Would wish. Would not be told
of the stink in the skull, the eye's collapse.
Would be told something new, something unknown.—
A mosquito bites my hand. The only sound
is the rough wind. Drunk I have been,
here, at the loam's maw, before this stone
of yours, which is not you. Which is.

The Lover Remembereth Such as He Sometime Enjoyed
And Showeth How He Would Like to Enjoy Her Again

Luck is something I do not understand:
There were a lot of things I almost did
Last night. I almost went to hear a band
Down at The Swinging Door. I, almost, hid
Out in my room all night and read a book,
The Sot-Weed Factor, that I'd read before;
Almost, I drank a pint of Sunny Brook
I'd bought at the Dickson Street Liquor Store.

Instead I went to the Restaurant-On-The-Corner,
And tried to write, and did drink a beer or two.
Then coming back from getting rid of the beer,
I suddenly found I was looking straight at you.
Five months, my love, since I last touched your hand.
Luck is something I do not understand.

Little Keats Soliloquy

You're probably wondering
what I'm doing with this
2-by-4 said a stableboy,
and when I came to with
dried blood in my ear
I knew that I had
missed the joke again.
It happens all the time:
that was no refried banana
that was my wife. That
means something? Meant nothing
to me while they grinned
their asses off. You go
straight to hell I said;
but I can't go through
life this way, always outside
watching the baker
plopping pastries into
sacks for other kids,
that's no good, I know
that for sure, but what
can I do, what can I
use for a ladder, what
to carry me up into
the loft, away from these
stinking horses?

The Murder of Gonzago and His Friends

In a district that's rarely traveled these days,
in a place where even the blackbirds lie down
in daylight, just north of West Fork,
I fell out with eight debauchees below some sycamores.
"Good fellows, arise!" I cried. "I
suspect you have heard the sad news."
But they were dull, sluggard, adamant, insane.
And besides, Mogen David seemed their chief concern.
The Arapahoes would soon be upon us: "Arise! Arise!
Shall blood-purple be the color of our pain?"
Nothing. Their eyes were not white rapids.
But no one could say I did not try. No one felt
I was to blame. No one. This was many years ago.
At night now, when I leave the house
with my jar of salt, my thoughts are of them. Each night
as I stand under my streetlight, I can think
only of them. And as I look down the long row
of streetlights, each with its own person,
holding his own jar, as I stand there
pouring salt on the slugs, that then blister and foam,
as I watch them dissolve, my thoughts are always of them.

Day Begins at Governor's Square Mall

Here, newness is all. Or almost all. And like
a platterful of pope's noses at a White House dinner,
I exist apart. But these trees now—
how do you suppose they grow this high in here?
They look a little like the trees I sat beneath in 1959
waiting with my cheesecloth net for butterflies.
It was August and it was hot. Late summer,
yes, but already the leaves in trees were
flecked with ochers and the umbers of the dead.
I sweated there for hours, so driven,
so immersed in the forest's shimmering life,
that I could will my anxious self not move
for half a day—just on the imagined chance
of making some slight part of it my own.
Then they came. One perfect pair of just-hatched
black-and-white striped butterflies. The white
lemon-tipped with light, in shade
then out, meandering. Zebra swallowtails,
floating, drunk in the sun, so rare to find
their narrow, fragile, two-inch tails intact.
At that moment I could only drop my net and stare.
The last of August. 1959. But these trees, now,
climb up through air and concrete never hot or cold.
And I suspect the last lepidoptera that found
themselves in here were sprayed then swept away.
Everyone is waiting though, as before a storm—
anticipating something. Do these leaves never fall?

Now, and with a mild surprise, faint
music falls. But no shop breaks open yet.
The people, like myself, range aimlessly;
the air seems thick and still. Then, lights blink on;
the escalators jerk and hum. And in the center, at
the exact center of the mall, a jet of water spurts
twenty feet straight up, then drops and spatters

14

in a shallow pool where signs announce that none
may ever go. O bright communion! O new cathedral!
where the appetitious, the impure, the old, the young,
the bored, the lost, the dumb, with wide dilated eyes
advance with offerings to be absolved and be made clean.
Now, the lime-lit chainlink fronts from over one hundred
pleasant and convenient stalls and stores are rolled away.
Now, odors of frying won tons come wafting up from
Lucy Ho's Bamboo Garden. And this music, always
everywhere, yet also somehow strangely played as if
not to be heard, pours its soft harangue down now.
The people wander forward now. And the world begins.

Deep Silence

Something wanders through my father's house
Dragging its chains. A discerning eye can see
It watching enormous amounts of daytime TV.
Of a morning, it eats corn flakes or bran flakes;
It sucks on penny candy. Its memory, I
Am sorry to say, is not what it used to be.

I have thought of selling admission to this.
For surely many people would pay to see
Such wonderful proofs of the supernatural,
Of how things just continue on.
                              Each day
It stumbles from one room to the next room,
Lifting its head up, its hands out, showing,
To the discerning eye, a solitary shaking
Of the chains from which it begs to be set free.

If I Could Open You

If I could open you, like
Einstein opened a hole
in the twentieth century,
that is what I would do.
When he realized what he
had done, I like to think he
sat there with his pencil, and
in his mind was a great, silver
city on a plain, and three
blue suns in the sky. And he
walked into that image then,
glad though terrified.

The Drifting Away of All We Once Held Essential

Now here's the truth: there is a tide in the affairs
of men. And it will drag your ass right out
to sea and dump you, if you aren't careful.
In October, in Texas, in a room, in a city,
the stylist sat, working on his book, *Strange
Things Along the Rio Grande*, a comparative study of
masturbatory techniques and tendencies of
certain southern oral-interpretation-of-literature
professors and South Texas redneck barflies.
But a seemingly insurmountable impasse
has been reached in the project, of late,
due to the almost complete refusal of
the barflies to answer the more pertinent portions
of his questionnaire. God! God! It all at once
made him think somehow, he knew not how,
of the day when he was just a jerk of a lad:
a page, a pup, a whelp, a wag, a sprite, a recent
winner of the Baby Leroy Look-Alike Contest, and he had
asked the doctor where these latest acquisitions, these
hemorrhoids, had come from. And he, misunderstanding,
thought the doctor said he must have recently had
a *hard stew*. And the doctor laughed laughed laughed
in his face, upon hearing him reply that he
hadn't had any stew at all in months. It, all at once,
made him think of kleptomania somehow, and what
a joy it had been to him in his younger days.
Question: is it true that, when the stylist
was thirteen, he had taken the whole fourteen dollars
he had made from selling Boy Scout peanut brittle
and spent it in one afternoon at the movies,
returning home with only a giant glue-together
plastic model of a bumblebee, some already fading
memories of the cyclops in *The Seventh
Voyage of Sinbad*, and the blood sugar level
of a terminal alcoholic, caused by

washing down eleven candy bars with three
chocolate malts? And is it also true that, one week
later, on their drive to the scout meeting
where the previously mentioned funds were to be
turned in, the child stylist informed his father
of what he had done, thus causing his father
to become distressed? Thus causing his father
to almost cry, saying over and over, "What did
we do wrong? What did we do wrong?" And
is it not the case that the child did
cry at that point in time, but in ecstasy,
as the father lent him the money he needed,
as they drove along, the child crying there beside him
in the dark? Answer: yes, all that's just as real
as a red rag; and it marvels the stylist, to this day,
with what complete vividness that scene, from
so many years gone by, can be called up for purposes
of flagellation, from the darker regions
to rip and tear at the pink soft underbelly of thought.
Look at them there: father and son, driving
along. So close. Real pals. My
God! What a load of crap! Kleptomania! Fuck! Shit!
Cunt! Piss! A whole family of Lone Rangers! That's
what it was! Masked Avengers! The William Tell
Overture ad infinitum. We flew our flag: *Don't
Tread On Me*. And if you did, then you'd see
such venom. I will do such things! I will steal
such things! What they are I know not. But I do know
Hold me Daddy and whip me Daddy, and turn
your distant eyes at last on me. See, I did
this and took this and this. Hold me. . . .
The stylist paused. Put down his pen. His eyes ran
dry. Tired. His mind was tired. But there was so much
still to do. He really had so very much to do.
He really must finish this latest project, this
attempt to add to the body of total knowledge in the world.

This Print of Dürer's

In this print of Dürer's hanging on the wall
The knight and horse are old but very strong;
The lines run down his face, his body clothed
Completely in thick armor that he loves.
His friend, a dog, runs gladly at his heel,
And they'll crush skulls before the day is gone.
Behind him loom monsters and monstrosities
That he's absorbed, or beaten, either way.

And Death arrives. His face sits on his sleeve,
An hourglass in his hand. The knight—
Is not afraid. No doubt he knows his way.
And there, see, on a hill, the furthest thing
Away, already passed, but visible, stand
The towers of a town where peace might be.

Morning Song

Flush and burn, your fever rose all night.
Your sleep was troubled; and even though I knew
This had to run its course, throughout the night
I tried but could not think of anything to do.
Often you cried out in that sleep, far away.
And wherever you were, I thought I could see
That whatever it was you kept wanting to say
It did not seem to have to do with me.

The tired eyes open. You see now that I see,
Swirling and tangled, inverted, how
In this firmament the blood streams and races.
Your smile and damp hair rush up to meet me,
Or is it I to them? This skin's blaze and glow—
The beads of dew on these most secret places.

This Other

Your self confronts you at the oddest times.
    Not too often, but often at odd times,
this other bangs through the front door, catching
    you tired and at supper, but still in your black
cape and doublet, tired, of imagining
    knowing, of imagining gesturing
hypnotically from the battlements,—
    and your dinner becomes an interrupted
dinner, as he sits down and digs into
    the roast duck, orange sauce, the red Bordeaux.

You think: what a strange fellow. A healthy
    appetite, but the little paper pirate hat
sitting on his head, the kind in the dime stores
    around Halloween, would put most people off.
He eats with his hands. Quickly. And yet,
    there is something about this ruffian,
something about this greasy gorilla,
    something about this person with a penchant
for orange sauce, that makes you think: here is one
    with which I might dine; one with which I might
lift a fine glass; one with which I might speak.

What It Feels Like to Live in This Country to Me

Where are all those yucks? With a more silent nature
than that of the corpse's fingernail stretching out
on the silk, up from the sea of stone, the sea
from which thought does not arise, an emotion
is headed our way. And speaking of fingernails,
I saw a movie once where they buried this guy
alive, because they thought he was dead. He wasn't. Later on,
they dug him up and he was. Fingernails, stubs, had raked
that coffin lid until it was streaked, smeared. He
wanted out, see. What could be more plain? Ah, now,
the guiding light is followed by the edge of night,
has been for years, and this experience, myself,
me and the television I'm observing at this
very minute, Bob Hope, with the sound off, bid a fond
farewell, to paraphrase Rilke somewhat loosely,
from the ballroom of the ambiguously blessed, and
O those cards and O those letters, communication,
reason is where it's at, but, as I said
with considerable power, in another poem
of my own making, Where is it?, who knows,
and to be quite honest, who gives a shit, what did I
just say?, Huntz Hall be with me till I end my song,
the log has been flogged behind the gray barn now,
out there, where snow is embraced gently by the earth,
where the earth is soaked from all that embracing, where
there is only a speck left, that's where it's at
after all, yes sir, just a dot, a raft at sea,
undefined, no distinguishing marks, the last placebo,
fading away like a stain into the realms of rue.

A Skeptical View of the Tarot

The Purveyor to the Czar attended a new exhibition
of post-impressionist efforts by Lonzo,
a recent twinkle in the art world sky.
The important official paused before
one painting, and said it gave *him*
the impression of the dried egg yellow
he found on his fork at breakfast that morning.
The next canvas, he said, gave him the impression
of his courtesan's black lace panties
lying on the carpet that afternoon,
a sour fog hovering over them, almost visible.

Lonzo, holding a skeptical view of the Tarot,
having, for the occasion, arrayed himself as The Fool
carrying a white rose and stolling over a cliff,
an ironic gesture of defiance,
heard these things.

As the purveyor continued his ridicule,
moving from painting to painting,
the locked stalls of the flaming mules
of melancholy were opened wide,
causing horrible screams to be heard in the land.
Then the artist was filled with dark choler,
saw the flaw in his gesture, and considered
that perhaps, after all, his chosen garb
did correctly express his archetype.

Chance of Showers

for Matt Horan

Like the greatest steak house
salad bar you ever saw, there is some-
    thing varied but, I am afraid, all
too familiar in this big autumnal air.

And yet, what other season
boils up such aches to get it down
    precisely, hoping to avoid again
the always striking, but also fatal,

    mention of the ornithological
V's on high. The trees seem the color
    of fire trucks or blood or rust
again, but why? Why do we recall

    the things we do? "Why did
the little moron take hay to bed?" I
    don't suppose a week has passed
in thirty years I have not asked myself

    that question. Why? Like-
wise with Billy Pinzer. I was only
    two, but every week I waddle out
on the porch once more, and see Billy

    in the front yard, holding a little
yellow metal roadster. Ah Billy, he is
    my buddy. He smiles at me. I
smile at him. I walk up to him. He hits

    me in the face with the roadster.
Sometimes, when I peer out at my freshman
    class, those seats of desolation,
or when I hear some Texan say something

particularly inane, I think
Billy is behind these bombs bursting
    in here that, for an instant,
cause me to consider flipping through

    advertisements in the back
of *Argosy*—to order a used, an actual
    Colombian machete. "Imagine
the expressions on your friends' faces

    as you cut a bloody swathe
through the gang." For an instant.
    Then I take another sip of coffee,
lean back and keep my mouth quite shut.

    So does form give meaning
to memory. Does memory give meaning
    to form? "Why yes!" cried crazy
Vera so long ago her face flared up

    today from some recess where I
thought just narcosis reigned, miasmal
    and malign. I got older this year,
and like black lightning from a blue sky

    it surprised the hell out
of me. I don't think I could honestly
    describe things as looking up,
but I can say they are still looking

    not dull. Mortality, who
would have thought it? Maybe the best
    to be hoped for is to pop off
in mid-melody, like Bach. These random

    cameos, however, and tableaux
on parade appear preferable to even
    the best of last refrains now.
For now. Now this glass wherein I see

myself lets me see other things
as well. That window in the far
	wall, for instance, and outside
houses dripping gingerbread on the hill

	across the street. If I squint
hard enough, they seem a rocky misty
	blue-gray panorama, like
·the inaccessible backgrounds of certain

	Renaissance portraits of great
renown. Although I must say those craggy
	backgrounds always made me think:
"That girl had better get going if she

	wants to be home by dark."
Hogs are among us, no doubt about it,
	no hedge against inflation
either. Ben Kimpel tells me things come

	in cycles, I suppose that means
circles, and I guess that is a type
	of good news, but I don't know, these
recollections seem constant, growing, one

	long craggy protean scene,
and my bad knee gets worse every year,
	I use it to forecast the weather
now, stuff to feed my nightmares and

	daymares. My parents singing
"Always." While the shish kebab sellers,
	on the corners and streets
of the world, are not moved to tears.

Robert Rickert Wrote Back

the roll, the rise, the carol . . .
HOPKINS

Robert Rickert wrote back, saying,
"Too many dead days in a row? Dost thou

not dwell near the sea? Shut up. Take
walks by the shore. Jesus. Get out.

Spend time beneath trees." And so today
I walked on the beach. And the clouds

out over the sea made the sea look
like one, enormous, heaving mass

of impure mercury. I thought, "How
lovely." And then, "How lovely to say

lovely." "It heaps me!" I claimed.
Then the dream came. A gargoyle

facing my face. My arm striking hard.
Carving. Let me cut the flare of this

nostril right! Deep shoulder pain.
Chips of gray stone in my hair. Birds

whirling round. My self on a rock roof
one hundred feet above ground. Let

me carve this flare! Face powdered
with stone dust and now rain beginning

beginning to cake my hair. But nothing
mattering but the flare. The ache

clean, cut clean, rain clean. The
flare! Then the gargoyle gives out,

retches rain from the spout of its mouth,
down over tongue and teeth, down

crashing and washing my face, my hair.
And that was the end. End of the dream.

Was all.— I came back to the beach.
Back to the soft, meaningless mantra,

the tide at my feet. Today, by the shore.
An unction. A dream of waking. To confront

and carve stone. Make mirrors in stone.
Gargoyles only some god would ever see.

Gifts

They say that blood is salt. I've
tasted yours, and they are right.
So let's get on with our big painting
exchange. In mine, I've placed you
in a black pasture, with black horses,
your red eyes clearly discerned. But,
and I observe you're having the same
problem, here in the middle distance
isn't really the right place for you
somehow. Over more to the left,
I think, yes, under that smeared vision
of crows, way out in those dark, waist-high
weeds, there, leaning against that
huge pile of horseshit, yes, and a little
nearer the vanishing point, thank you.

To All Those Considering Coming to Fayetteville

Often these days, when my mind holds splinters
like the pieces of the Old Spice bottle
I dropped and shattered yesterday, I think
of other places. It is wintertime now,
and the Ozarks are hushed up with snow
everywhere. They are small mountains, almost
not mountains at all, but rather, with trees
sticking up, they seem more like
the white hairy bellies of fat old men
who have lain down here. What has this to do
with anything? I don't know. Except
it makes me think of snow elsewhere, and what
it would be like to be there. I might drive
across Oklahoma, then on into
New Mexico. I could be there tonight.
The land would be flat, the snow over
everything. The highway straight, and forever
the snow like blue cheese in the moonlight,
for as far as there is, and air, cold air
crisp as lettuce, wet lettuce in the store,
and I would keep driving, on and on.

Semi-Sentimental Thank You Note
Sent Over a Long Distance

Let me tell you, I'm
    still trying to cope with
the disappointment. All I
    wanted for Christmas was
a scratch-and-sniff photo
    of you amongst some
clover. Instead, this book
    of the fifty worst
movies ever made. And
    a box of pink erasers?
Maybe I'm slow but I
    don't get it. Oh yes, I
know we are separated by
    that enormously faded
and dirty spread-out
    serape, that distinctive
state of mind, Oklahoma.
    But down here I am
left mostly to my own
    devices. Here, like Jackie
Gleason's red satin bowling
    shirt, I lack subtlety
and stand too much out
    in the crowd. So what I
am getting at, what I am
    trying to say, my
little lotus blossom, my
    little dove of Canaan, my
little garbanzo bean, is
    thanks a lot, but I
really must ask you
    to get up off that
divine rotundity, your
    ass, and send that clever

clover photo right on down
   the line right now. There
exists a definite need!
   Like Jackie Gleason's bowling
shirt, sooner or later, I'm
   headed your way, and when
I get back to Arkansas,
   either to pick you up
or stay, let's both plan on
   working hard at, O ho,
seeing, ah, eye to eye, et
   al, and I might add, toe
to toe, et al, nose to
   nose, O, thigh to thigh,
et al, ah, O, well, yes, O.

Wakulla Springs

Three and a half dollars
for The Covered Boat Jungle Cruise
to see "The Alligator In His Natural Habitat"
and the "Actual Site"
of the "On-Location Filming"
of *The Creature From The Black Lagoon*
seemed a real deal to my wife and me.

Except that the guide
of The Covered Boat Jungle Cruise
kept repeating into his microphone:
Now up here on your right you got your gator.
That one there being Oh about
two hundred year old, by my recknin'.
Now up here on your left. . . .
And, by my count, nine separate times saying:
Now up here on your left you got
your anhinga! Fabled fowl!
Snakebird or water turkey! Anhinga!
Gotta sit and spread them wings to dry—
before he can fly!
And the mother on the bench behind us:
Cissy. Be careful. Cissy.
Cissy. Leave the man's hair alone, Cissy.
Cissy! Now aren't you ashamed.

Deep, dark green water.
Frayed beards of Spanish moss
hanging from the cypress trees.
An osprey floating through a crystal sky.
And the anhinga,
                    . . . Fabled fowl!
Snakebird or water turkey. . . .
He must sit still just a little longer
before he can fly away.

Often in Different Landscapes

What should be done? No one knew for sure.
"Look at that chili-dog," I said to the blind guy,
after which I took it on the lam. The entire
offended countryside was up in arms. *The Scourge
of Sheboygan* the media labeled me. Those swine,
they forced me to the forests, taking shelter
in an abandoned hunting lodge. And only sometimes,
on the weekends, would I hear the snickering sounds
of couples in the woods. That first night, that
lonely night, the sleep dripped from my eyes,
was replaced by more, and rain dripped, and the dark
with its hard tonnage, I should add, also dripped,
oozing like hot asphalt under the door. Why
did it remind me so much of the blind guy
and his constant drool? My gorge rose. But not
for long. I packed those days with simple things,
taking up the Ace comb with cellophane, playing
songs of my own invention, such as "Johnny Belinda
Where Is Thy Sting," a personal favorite. But that, too,
sometimes brought thoughts of the blind guy, why
I don't know. And neither do I understand
where these recurring images come from, strange
images, often in different landscapes, and always
coming back, huge indigestions, to glut
my sleep, my waking moments, all my life
clogged with glossolalia, white canes, shrieks, slobber,
the spastic I tripped once behind the gym.

The Lamar Tech Football Team Has Won Its Game

The Lamar Tech football team has won its game.
My grandmother has died. The newspaper, yesterday,
said, "Siamese Twins Cut Apart, One Lives." My father
says, "Some things you have to learn to accept.
Take the good parts with the bad."
                                    (This must be a dream.)
"Oh, yes," I say. "I remember how the sun feels warm
even on the coldest days, sometimes."
The Lamar Tech football team.   The newspaper.

Belgium is now importing jukeboxes.
Australians are installing oil heaters.
Adversity is what makes you mature. "Oh, yes.
I've seen the winter moon pumped up, platinum-like;
and the stars *seem* brightest when it's freezing."
Siamese twins.   On the coldest days, sometimes.
                                    (This must be a dream.)
My father says, "Make hay while the sun shines."
The sun.   The moon.   Belgium is now importing
jukeboxes.   One lives.   My father says, "In a few weeks
you'll feel better. Time is a great healer."   The sun.
The moon.
The Lamar Tech football team has won its game.

Summer in Fairbanks

is like a dull dream. From time to time
the paper boy comes grinning with proof that
something has happened after all. Here
where the highways end. To go north
from here, you must be a bird or wealthy.
The prospectors have each been starved and strained
away down southward and to old folks homes.
Here is where the nights end too. Never
to sense the dark for days is strange, and not
so hot as one might think. It is strange
always to be able to see, and say:
that is there and that is there and that
is over there, always. Strange, not to tell
the end of days by any other way
than clocks, and meals; televisions turning off.
Different, for things to seem
to the eyes like one day, that somehow
has slowed down to months, years, icebergs
of minutes so separated by an absence
from anything that ever came before,
that the anxious people find themselves
waiting for the swish on their lime lawns
of the dirty tennis shoes of
the grinning paper boy who brings them yesterday.

The North Slope

Three months away from the word away from trees
and bushes hills newspapers women dark
on into the undeodorized the raw
twelve hours a day seven days a week
helicopters dropped us on tundra unrelieved
abandoned well sites to do away with
anything "environmentally unsound" there that
first day stacking scrap metal thinking the last words
of Scarlett O'Hara seeing how flat
the land was how brown how completely
unrelieved the flatness how raw the air
coming off the Arctic sea the horizon
a pencil line sometimes blending
with the frigid summer sky unrelieved
a foot and a half of tundra and under it
ice going down frozen earth eighteen hundred feet
I remember the small tundra flowers
delicate white blue the yellow poppies
in the second week I reached out to pick some
saw a jut of ice beside them
reaching up strange I shivered strange
something there I did not quite understand
could not get my mind around something
ice underneath them then back at base camp
before bed thought again and again
coldness what is it I thought strange unrelieved
more and more could not look at the flat
horizon or would not would keep my gaze away
from the white sky white fog the white
light from the sun never sinking what is it
I did not know only this feeling
someone walking always away something unsaid
and I kept my head down away from the sun the sky
then came the week of the caribou
the herds they came running unrelieved

thousands and thousands across the tundra
I kept my head down but at last could not
a hundred yards away two wolves loping behind
I saw them drag down a slow one
it was one hundred yards away
I saw them could not believe saw them
the red meadow of its side this was
one hundred yards away watched them eat
there was ice underground is ice
underground could not believe saw them rip ice
from its side ice the color of the sun I saw
it was raw it was nothing that fell from
its side ice emptiness came loping as birds
so many birds flew away and away screaming over
something they seemed to have heard
unrelieved the sound now of blood falling
of ice now and of whaleboats I could not believe
thinking her last words what was it the birds said
going away what was it the ice whispered raw
could not lift my head
the jet trails sagged over Dead Horse
and drifted away here where you aim
the harpoon sailor see it surface see it wallow
unrelieved see it dive here where the wait is
the ache for anything anything not dropping away
she breaches she breaches they cried and that
image charging my head all that white reaching
up that vacuum revealed unrelieved
and the froth all the spray and it sinking back
under leaving me asking for some other thing
for some other way asking time
to turn to forget what is there what is not
everywhere birds kept flying away
but Scarlett Scarlett this is the place
where tomorrow never comes the sun like
red ice searing always the summer the land
of absence of nothing of cold of no night
the wind blowing frozen off the Arctic sea

A Few Words for Frank Stanford: 1948–1978

We live awhile. And then
   we die. "The first
time I saw you, I thought
   you was bald," he said
to me. I checked my head,
   to see if he was right.

Of all things to recall
   on this first birthday
of this death, that was
   the first to come along.

1. *The Tale*
Back when a few of us others would gather together,
the red steaks on, the cheap wine rolling down,
we would tell the true, the oft-repeated story
of the summer Frank worked on Sam's surveying crew.

   One day they stopped for lunch out in the woods
   where they had been clearing brush almost since dawn.
   After a while, Frank jumped up with no warning,
   stripped, grabbed his machete and ran off into the trees
   hacking, screaming, over and over, "I
   am physically superior! Mentally superior! I
   am spiritually superior to anybody here!"
   Now, the ones who happened to be *there*
   were Sam, and two semi-illiterates sucking Skoal.
   One spit, and said, "That boy is a weird one.
   You got to admit he's a hell of a worker though."

And then we'd laugh and drink, devour, and drink
some more. Laughter and liquor seemed much the same

back then. Each of us cramming deep inside the fact
that possibly Frank had meant some other thing:
that possibly Frank had attempted to convey
that when he said *here*, he didn't mean *there*, but
here, us, with our wine. And the thing that stung
in our little selves, our so young selves,
our enormous, ignorant, frightened selves:
we thought possibly what he had to say was true,—
or, more than that, maybe, possibly, probably, true.

2. *His House*
It fell to us to clean the sick mess up,—
so we drove over, slid up into his yard
and parked the car. The honeysuckle stank.
The door was open and every light was on.
It looked like somebody had left in a hurry:
the house was empty, but every light was on.

There was a little blood on the bed, a little
blood smeared on the phone and that was all.
The house was empty. We stood around.
                                        Frank,
while I was flying back from Houston
you effected a definite, permanent change,
and every light was on. This was the home
where a man had taken a gun and blown and blown
and blown his being away three hours before.
I never knew what silence was, Frank,
until I walked through that door.

3.

He cared for *Wise Blood.*
    He cared for Cocteau.
For *Rashomon.* A man obsessed
    by his own adoption,
"There are two people
    inside of me," he said.
"I don't know who I am," he
    told me, drunk and sad,—
but not, I think, entirely so.

He acquired, through the years,
    devoted disciples not
to be denied. Near the end,
    when he was in debt, when he
thought he was immortal,
    when he had arrived
at a country where
    others could scream and
call and he could not
    hear, there, near the end,
near that ragged, barren,
    ignorant, excessive end,
we did not get along. But
    I feel now I must say:
"When he sat down at a desk
    the juice crackled and came.
He could write about
    moonlight. He could write
about swine. He could
    write about starfish,
lunchmeat, Memphis,
    minnows and bay rum,

Robert Desnos. He had
    the blue flow. He had
the red hand. My God,
    he had the touch, my friends."

Those are the final words
    on this ridiculous day:
he had the touch, my friends.
    When a world winds down
there need be none but those.
    Never, never, never,
no words but those. Except
    perhaps, "We live awhile."

So, bring women to sing,
    and to cover him over
with white sheets of paper.

Bring roses to deaden
    the clods as they fall.

Sometimes

Sometimes in summer, I lie in bed, just
at dawn, and outside my window I
see the morning strike the trees' leaves
in a way that lets me blur my sight, until
I see, not trees, but canyons of yellow
and green; or, if not canyons, water then,
maybe water falling, with the sun's glint
glancing off, as it does off spray, or it
could be white lava, or green. Then the day.

Airport Bars

1.
Like shoveling in linguini
while listening to *Bolero*
at dinner last night,
and like pouring down White Russians
between flights tonight,
things are gaining speed.

In the rain outside,
they taxi, roll and rise.

Does everything always depart
and does nothing remain?

These big windows, and the way
the wind flings its wet against them,
the way, far down, people outside
are blown around in silence,
the way their flashlights flicker on
then off, in silence, blinking
asterisks in blackness, and how
the people speak in silence,
the lips move, but without sound,
reminds me, for a moment,
of a silent film I saw once
called *Orphans of the Storm*.
But only for a moment, then—
it goes.
Pouring down White Russians.

Do memories always depart?
It seemed that in that movie
people were always buffeted about
by great but natural forces,

when all they really wanted—
and not with much success—
was to hold their ground,
or get back to where they came from,
or make a little headway
toward some vaguely distant town
over the horizon.

Where are the peach-tinted sunsets,
the green summer twilights,
those sidewalks on which
I smeared *JANE POSHATASKE*
in lightning bug, luminous,
chartreuse, phosphor, fading away?
God, the things that return,
that we wish would remain,
like resurrected Romanovs
laying claim for a while
to a throne long gone, but they fade—
pinpoints of light, they fade,
stains on the dark, they fade,
leaving only the far, slate wall
of what is still to be. And that wall
is speeding up. It is moving this way.

2.
And if memories stayed? How would that be?
Cautiously,
carefully, of such should we dream,
for most of the time
welling up, come back things
that seem more like Shakespearean ghosts
than like twilights, golden or green,
ghosts full of prophecy, banshees, old trolls

46

with gnarled knuckles, grabbing hold
and being loath to let go—
fungi, of sorts, but no,
almost never those beautiful twilights.
Of that I am sure.

3.
It was one of those
"Golden Age" TV variety hours
that started each week with caricatures
of twenty or thirty of the biggest stars
distorted but recognizably drawn—
then each week one or two would appear.

Martha Raye's mouth was as big
as her head, but it was
JIMMY DURANTE
that caught his eye—
because in the rendering the artist had done
JIMMY DURANTE
had a sausage for a nose,
a foot-long sausage, fat and round.

He asked his father if that was so.
"Oh, Jesus yes:
JIMMY DURANTE
has a huge nose."

And so the boy felt, "If somewhere that
could somehow be—
well, maybe the world really is a wonder—
and not what it seems."

Then the night they announced that the host that week
would be The-One-And-Only!
Mr. Ink-A-Dink-A-Doo!
The Old Schnozzola!
a rush of joy
slid along his spine—
and a soft, slow thunder wandered through his mind.

Then this ugly old guy danced out—
and at that exact instant
a glimpse of The Essence
was portioned out
for the boy to see:
a loud old man, a total ass.
But no sausage anywhere to be seen.

His father looked over,
noticed the frown,
the reek, the faint auras
of disgust and disappointment
swirling.

"Ha ha!" the father said, "Close,
but no kielbasa. Ha ha!" the father said,
"Close, but no cigar."

4.
And so we sit here, Gentle Reader,
halfway between two places,
looking for a little satinity
to ease the slide;
not knowing anyone
for many miles around,

but feeling, for no discernible cause,
My Gracious Peruser-Of-This-Page,
an inability to be laid-back about it,
the same self-consciousness a man feels
when he finds himself alone in a room,
swilling down White Russians,
and begins to act out
all the things he might have said.
Then someone comes in, stands behind him,
catching him there with his finger in the air.

The Party's End

The moon steered a rusty car away.

We wandered into the backyard.

There was a little wind.

Someone sad whispered, "See,
now the poem of joy comes striding."

And I saw it then.

Why did it come then,
through the dirty horse of the night?

What visions came?

I saw my father working.
He bent and fell in Alaskan snow.

My brother also fell.

I wanted to touch them then.
I believe
I wanted to scream, "Help me, God!
Immensity!
Let me come unto you!
Let me come unto you!
Let me come unto you!"

But, of course,
none of us said anything.

The dawn was there.

And I was cold.
And all rage left me.

A frost had collected
on the shingles, and the grass,
so lovely
to my drunken eyes.

To His Book

Wafer; thin and hard and bitter pill I
   Take from time to time; pillow I have lain
      Too long on; holding the brief dreams, the styled
Dreams, the nightmares, shadows, red flames high
   High up on mountains; wilted zinnias, rain
      On dust, and great weight, the dead dog, and wild
Onions; mastodonic woman who knows how,—
   I'm tired of you, tired of your insane
      Acid eating in the brain. Sharp stones, piled
Particularly, I let you go. Sink, or float, or fly now,
                Bad child.

The Man Who Burnt Bridges

Like an old Ethel Waters 78 of "Stormy Weather,"
poor whites, poor blacks, drunks, and thieves
cried out in the streets all night. And when I woke,
to margarine-colored walls and water stains
like Rorschachs on the ceiling, I still could hear
them moan. They were real. The wars against
gravity would not be won there, I could tell.
And so I left, and as I left I once again burnt bridges.

Hard winds and rains back there brought many down.
This wind is cold. It pricks and stings. It singes
the skin of me, the man of mode, impervious to
irony. I shrug. Shake. Then wrap this habit round.
How fresh and exquisite the far horizon seems.